A Day Off

Pictures by **Ray Cruz**

G. P. Putnam's Sons · New York

A Day Off

by Tobi Tobias

Fourth Impression

Text copyright © 1973 by Tobi Tobias
Illustrations copyright © 1973 by Ray Cruz
All rights reserved. Published simultaneously in
Canada by Longmans Canada Limited, Toronto.

SBN: GB-399-60762-5
SBN: TR-399-20268-4

Library of Congress Catalog Card Number: 72-84839
PRINTED IN THE UNITED STATES OF AMERICA
06209

for John and Anne,
with love and chicken soup

About once a year, usually in that part of the winter when the snow's all turned to slush and the sun hasn't poked out of that gray sky for days and days, I like to be sick, but not very.

Just a *little* sick. Like a cold maybe or a small stomachache. Just sick enough not to go to school today . . .

but not medicine sick, not doctor sick. Just
sick enough to get back into bed after breakfast
all nice and warm and lazy.

Not so sick that my mother gets her worrying look when she sees my temperature on the thermometer . . .

but sick enough so it's me she's fussing over
today and not my dumb baby brother.

Not too sick to spread out all my baseball
cards on the bed so I can sort out my collection.
It's the greatest . . .

but much too sick to pick them up and put
them all away.

Not too sick to watch a little extra TV . . .

but sick enough to watch lying on the couch,
with my pillow and blanket.

Sick enough to stay in my pajamas all day
and not get dressed . . .

but not sick enough to need a robe and
slippers for going to the bathroom. And maybe,
as long as I'm in there, try a little toothpaste
writing on the mirror.

Sick enough for chicken soup and French toast and cherry Jello for lunch, on a tray, in bed . . .

but not so sick I can't have hamburgers and French fries with ketchup for dinner tonight, at the table with everyone else.

Sick enough for my daddy to call up from the
office to find out how I'm doing . . .

but not so sick I can't get up out of bed to talk
to him.

Sick enough not to be able to do my homework . . .

but not too sick to read my sister's three new
whopper comic books.

Sick enough to have a cup of tea with a
spoonful of honey stirred around in it, or ginger
ale with ice and a straw . . .

but not soft-boiled egg, yucky glasses of hot milk sick.

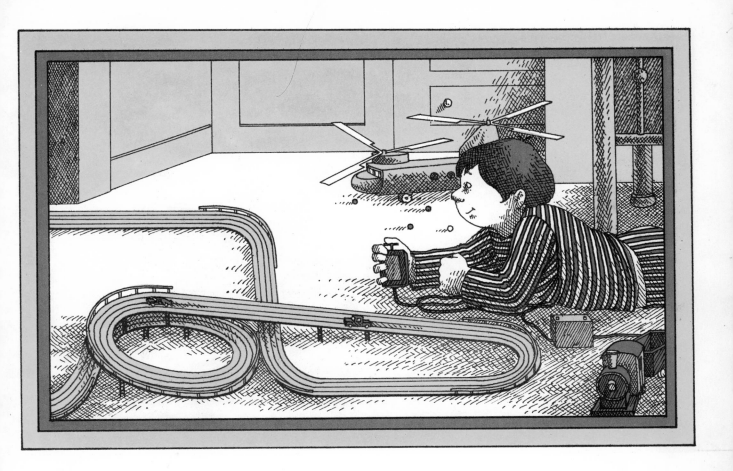

Not too sick to play with a few toys,

like my super action powered speedy wheels racing car set that's got over one mile of fit-together track—

and my gloopy plastic mold-it-yourself
monster-making machine—

and my giant interspace-parts
construction outfit you can build a
whole city of the future with—

That's the kind of sick I like to be, once in a while. Just a day off sick. And better, back to school, tomorrow.

The Author

When TOBI TOBIAS was nine, her
father said, "If you do anything at all,
you'll write." She was as good as his
word. She writes books for children
and articles for *Dance Magazine*,
where she is a Contributing Editor.
She has also become Irwin's wife, John
and Anne's mother, half-owner of a
half-renovated brownstone on New
York's Upper West Side, and a very
good cook.

The Artist

RAY CRUZ is a talented and versatile artist who loves children. He has done not only children's book illustrations, but textile and package design, murals, and advertising illustrations. Mr. Cruz lives in New York City and is involved in wildlife conservation and ecology. For Putnam's he has also illustrated *Jennifer Takes Over P.S. 94* by Mary Lystad, about which Kirkus Reviews said: "The droll pictures, of delightfully unprettified children stretching, shouting, fighting, parading, and partying, convey exuberance without being extravagant."